G-FORCE

THE MISUNDERSTOOD MOLE

Adapted by Sarah Nathan

Based on the screenplay by The Wibberleys and Ted Elliott & Terry Rossio and Tim Firth

Based on a story by Hoyt Yeatman

Executive Producers Mike Stenson, Chad Oman, Duncan Henderson, David James

Produced by Jerry Bruckheimer

Directed by Hoyt Yeatman

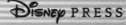

DISNEP PRESS

NEW YORK

CHAPTER
~ 1 ~

My name is Speckles. I'm a mole—the only mole on the G-Force. The G-Force is made up of three guinea pigs—Darwin, Blaster, and Juarez—and a fly named Mooch.

We are all highly trained secret agents.

Our first mission was simple: get inside a man named Leonard Saber's home and find a program called Project Clusterstorm.

A lot was riding on this mission. If we completed it successfully, we would finally be a real group of spies. If we failed, our team—the G-Force—would be disbanded.

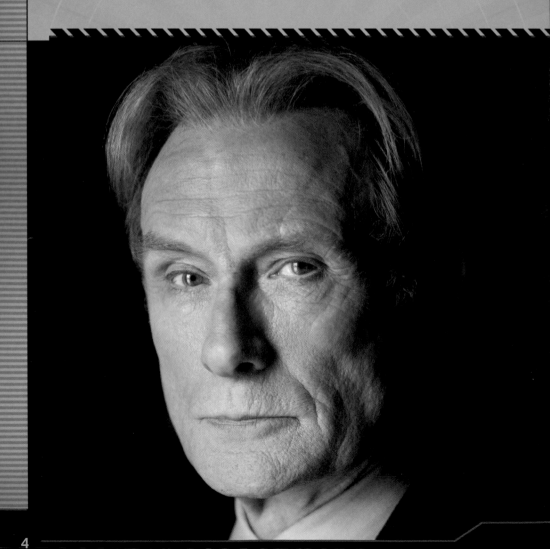

While the rest of the team entered from above, I stayed hidden underground. I used my computer to help guide Darwin, the team's leader, through the house. I wear thick glasses, but I'm still blind as a bat. Moles get around with our excellent senses of smell, touch, and hearing. My eyes don't slow me down. *Nothing* slows me down.

Leonard Saber ran a large company called Saberling Industries. They made household appliances. According to our information, they were also making secret weapons. The G-Force was supposed to figure out what kind of weapons.

Sure, I was working with the G-Force, but they weren't my friends. They didn't understand. They could *never* understand. But I just kept my head down and did my work. Soon they would know of my grand plan.

First, though, there was a mission to complete. "Darwin," I said over my headset, "you are clear to infiltrate Saber's study."

Safely inside, Darwin hacked into Saber's computer (with my help, of course). He copied the Clusterstorm file and hightailed it out of there.

I was supposed to use an escape tunnel to meet the rest of the team. But something was waiting for me at the end of the tunnel. A dog's mouth! "No escape," I told the others. "I repeat, no escape."

Blaster tried to save me—but he just made the dog mad and ended up stuck in a bush. It was Darwin and Juarez that came to my rescue. We were all safe—for now.

CHAPTER
-2-

Back at our headquarters, I quickly got to work. "Just a few more touches to decode Saber's crypto system," I told the others.

Ben, our human leader, was anxious to get the results. When I finally hacked into the file, the news was not good.

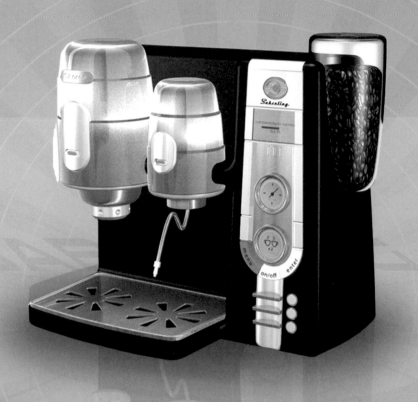

All we saw on the screen was a coffeemaker. We had failed!

Ben's boss demanded that the G-Force be taken into custody.

We had to get out of there—fast! We ducked into emergency escape tunnels and blasted out of Ben's house, the agents hot on our tails.

The rest of the team all rushed into a box for safety. But I wasn't about to get in a box—boxes are nothing but cages. "No!" I cried. "I don't do cages."

"Speckles, let's go!" Darwin yelled. It looked like I had no other option.

I was not happy in that box, and things got worse. The box was lifted up and placed in a bright room with many more cages. We were in a pet store! The only way out was to get adopted. I had little hope. Who would want a mole?

Blaster and Juarez were adopted almost immediately. But I had a plan! I played dead and the pet shop guy fell for it! But he didn't bring me outside as I had hoped. Instead, he threw me into a garbage truck. It was fine by me. Let the rest of the G-Force think I was gone. My master plan was shaping up very nicely. . . .

CHAPTER
-3-

My plan you ask? It was simple. I had created an alter ego by the name of Yanshu. Then I teamed up with Saber. But Saber didn't know who his partner really was! And he didn't know that when he launched Project Clusterstorm, my plan would be complete.

After I "escaped" from the pet store, I went to my control center, in the basement of Saber's house. There I sat viewing the TV screens and computers, and waited.

But I was in for a surprise. Darwin and his crew showed up in Saber's basement! The G-Force had all gotten out of the pet store and found their way to my hideout!

"Specks... *you* were behind all this?!" Darwin cried, stepping forward.

Darwin couldn't believe Clusterstorm was the result of just one clever mole with a computer.

"We thought you were dead, Specks," Darwin said. He sounded hurt. But I knew the truth.

"Like you really cared," I said. Behind me, I could hear my computers hard at work. Soon, it would begin. . . .

"Why are you doing this?" Darwin asked.

"Ever done a web search on the word mole?"
I asked. I had. There were over three million
entries—on how to kill us. Sure we might mess
up a golf course or two, but was that cause for
always making us the bad guys?

I was done explaining myself. I strapped myself into my seat. The ground began to shake, and then—I was lifted into the air. I had made an appliance monster in order to get my revenge!

It's too bad the G-Force was so determined. They grabbed on to cables and hung on.

But it didn't matter. Already, my program was working! Space debris was falling from the sky.

It was beautiful to see the humans running scared. I thought back to the day the exterminator came to my home, which was on a golf course. "Well, aren't you ugly?" the man had grumbled when he peered down into my hole.

I had always dreamed of the day I would have my revenge. And finally, that day had come! Not even the G-Force could stop me.

I leaned closer to the microphone. "Well, aren't you ugly!" I screamed to the people scurrying below.

Too bad the G-Force hadn't stayed in the pet store. And they had found a way to shut down my program—the extermination virus I had created. It was housed in a handheld device.

Just then, Mooch, that annoying fly, appeared. He was carrying the device! He skillfully dropped it into Darwin's paws. This was not good.

"Mooch, no!" I cried. The device would destroy everything!

CHAPTER

- 5 -

Darwin looked over at me. "Extermination viruses," he said as he slammed the device into a port. "Nasty stuff."

My command center began to crumble around me. "You spoiled everything," I said to Darwin. And then I slammed down to Earth.

Sure, the G-Force may have won this time.
Sure, Darwin transferred the virus to my system
and stopped Project Clusterstorm.

But I'm Speckles. I'm smarter than all those guinea pigs! I have a backup plan. The smart ones always do. So watch out! I'll be back!